Seasonal

NIGHT OF THE WHITE STAG

M. C. HELLDORFER

ILLUSTRATED BY YVONNE GILBERT

BLOOMSBURY
CHILDREN'S
BOOKS

BLOOMSBURY
CHILDREN'S
BOOKS

First published in Great Britain in 1999
Bloomsbury Publishing Plc, 38 Soho Square, London, W1V 5DF

First published in America in 1999
Random House, Inc., New York

Text copyright (c) Mary Claire Helldorfer 1999
Illustrations copyright (c) Yvonne Gilbert 1999
The moral right of the author and illustrator has been asserted

A CIP catalogue record of this book is available from the British Library
ISBN 0 7475 4606 1

Printed in Hong Kong/China

1 3 5 7 9 10 8 6 4 2

FOR THE ONE WHOSE LOVE IS MERCIFUL

—*M.C.H.*

TO THE MEMORY OF MY HUSBAND, DAVID,
AND MY DEAR FRIEND JOHN

—*Y.G.*

One cold Christmas Eve, when families huddled close to fires, a boy named Finder set out alone in a snowstorm. The king's war had ended the summer before, but Finder's father had never returned. Now his younger brothers and sisters were hungry. The family's fields lay burned and barren beneath the snow. Not a scrap of food was left in the house.

So Finder put on the cloak his father had once worn, belting it around him, for it was much too large. Around his neck he hung a ribbon with his father's gold ring, which bore the symbol of the old king.

"Stay on the road, child," his mother warned him. "Go straight to the king. Tell him your father was Lionel, who served him faithfully. When the king sees the ring, he will help us. He must!"

Finder followed the road, but only as far as the first curve. He knew a shorter path through the woods, a path where the royal hunters laid their traps. *Three fat rabbits will help my family more than scraps from the king,* he thought.

Whistling so that he'd feel a little braver, he entered the ice-webbed forest.

Finder hurried to the first trap. It was empty, its bait and rabbit snatched. The second trap also lay bare, except for bits of fur. The boy rushed on. At last he bent down and brushed back the snow; but the third trap was not where he had thought.

Now Finder turned around, no longer sure where he was. All he could hear was hissing snow. All he could see were dark slashes of trees against the whiteness. Suddenly a hand reached out and grasped him by the neck.

"Are you hunting, too?" an old man asked.

His long white beard was tangled with ice. Both hands gripped a spear, his fingertips glistening blue.

"I'm looking for rabbits, sir," Finder replied.

The old man shook his head. "This is the night of wonders," he said, "the night to hunt the great white stag."

Finder knew that no one had seen the white stag for a hundred years. And he saw how the man stared, his eyes like frosted moons.

"Are you lost, old father?" he asked gently. "Are you blind?"

"I have seen more than you ever want to see," the old man replied, "but nothing since the terrible war. You will be my guide, boy." He waved his spear. "To the hunt! To the hunt!"

Finder turned the old man around. He tried to lead him back to where he thought the road would be, but the hunter would not go that way.

"To the hunt, to the hunt!" he sang. Ignoring Finder's protests, he pulled the boy deeper and deeper into the forest. Finder, growing frightened, reached for his father's ring.

Suddenly the old man stopped.

"Listen," he said. "Do you hear it?"

Finder shivered. "I hear nothing."

The man pushed on, grasping Finder's arm so that he could not slip away.

"Listen, boy. Do you hear it now?"

"No, old hunter—"

"Listen," the old man pleaded. "Be my ears! For I have heard little since my son rode off in the thunder of war."

Finder stood very still. He heard it—inside him, like his own heartbeat: the pounding of strong, fast hooves.

"This way!" he said.

He and the old hunter hurried along as fast as possible, but they could not keep up. The hoofbeats faded. The old man leaned heavily on Finder.

"Stop," he said. "What do you smell?"

"Nothing, old hunter."

"Breathe deeply, boy."

Finder turned his head, then sighed. "There is nothing, sir."

"Breathe for me!" the old man cried. "For I have breathed nothing but cold and death since my son was wounded in the war."

Finder took a deep breath. The sweetness of new pine and traces of wood blossoms spiced the air. "I smell springtime," he said.

They followed the scent, travelling a long way to the frozen heart of the forest. Finder's bones ached with cold. Each step the old man took was slower than the last.

"Here," he said. "Do you see it?"

Finder looked about. "No," he said quietly. "There is nothing."

"Look again, boy," the old man said.

"I see nothing! Nothing!" Finder cried out, his stomach hollow with hunger and his fingers blue as the old man's.

"Be my eyes, boy, for I have seen nothing since the day I saw my only son killed in the war."

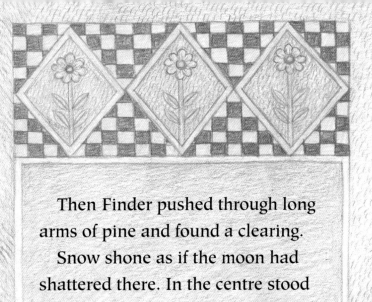

Then Finder pushed through long
arms of pine and found a clearing.

Snow shone as if the moon had
shattered there. In the centre stood
a great stag, whiter than the snow,
larger than any Finder had ever seen.
The stag gazed back at the boy. Its
eyes were dark and old as night,
gentle as love.

"You see it," said the old man.

"Some wonder!" whispered Finder.

"Point to it, child."

Finder did; then he lifted the old
man's arm, pointing the tip of his
trembling finger.

The hunter drew back with all his strength and hurled his spear.

Finder shouted and ran forward.

The great white stag took the spear's blow, leaped sideways, and disappeared. In the snow lay drops of scarlet.

"You tried to kill him!" Finder exclaimed.

"He was good," the hunter said, sinking down in the snow. "He was good, and everything good died in the war."

But Finder cried out still: "Look what you have done!"

He scooped up the pink snow and smeared it on the old man's eyes, as if he could make him see the blood his spear had drawn.

The old man blinked. His sight was restored, his eyes washed clear by the stag's blood. He reached for the gold ring around Finder's neck.

"Son of Lionel," he said, "your father served his king faithfully. So have you served me."

Together the hunter and Finder searched for the wounded stag, following its hoofprints in the snow. At the edge of the forest, the tracks vanished. A castle rose up before them.

"Go in," the old man said. "Ask to see the king and tell him of the marvel you have seen tonight."

"Come with me," Finder pleaded. "The king will not believe a boy. He will send me away with nothing for my family."

But the hunter would walk no further. He slipped through a small door in a snow-covered hill, leaving the boy alone.

Finder climbed to the castle entrance and showed the guards his father's ring. He was led to a great hall, cold as a tomb and sunken in shadows. At the far end, people stood silently while the king was helped to his throne.

Finder told his story quickly, then looked up. From beneath the golden crown, the old hunter's eyes gazed back at him.

"Welcome, son of Lionel," the king said. "You have your father's strong heart. This night, hunting with you, I have been given back mine."

The king descended to embrace Finder. When the king's people saw this, they knew he had been healed.

"The king sees again!" they exclaimed. "It is the white stag! A wondrous sign has been given to us!"

Candles were lit. Hearths and torches blazed. For the first time since the war had ended, the people sang and danced.

The king gave Finder food and many gifts, and a promise never to forget the needs of Lionel's family.

In the years that followed, the king remained true to his word. Both the boy's family and the kingdom grew strong again.

Sometimes, during the coldest weeks of those years, Finder would wake to hear pounding hooves circling his family's cottage. And once, on a night too windy and bitter for person or beast, he saw the white stag keeping watch from the woods, its eyes old as night and gentle as love.

SOURCE NOTES

In this tale you will find folkloric elements common to many cultures: animals that are helpful or redemptive figures, animals whose unusual white colour indicates power or sacredness, and hunters who quest after something far greater than the named beast.

Medieval literature in particular provided much of this story's imagery and inspiration. One obvious source is the legend of St. Eustace, later incorporated in St. Hubert's story, in which a saint goes hunting and has a vision of a stag with a cross between its horns. A subtler but more powerful influence is Chaucer's *Book of the Duchess*. In this elegy, a knight, struggling to deal with his wife's death, strays from a hunt, has a vision in which he finds consolation, then returns to court with new hope. Many medieval dream visions follow the narrative line I used—a suffering individual goes into the woods or wilderness, has a dreamlike experience, and returns to civilisation healed and strengthened—but Chaucer's is the one that moved me deeply and the one with which I now see the most specific connections.

The word *now* is important, because I did not have the *Book of the Duchess* consciously in mind when I wrote about Finder and the king. The catalyst for the tale was a meditation in a church bulletin, a few lines from the seventeenth-century Huron Carol, written by a French missionary for the Huron Indians. The image of hunters wandering in a forest on Christmas Eve was all I "remembered" as I wrote.

These many sources of ideas make me realize once more how fortunate we are as readers. When it comes time to work out the hardest stories of our lives, we have a treasury of images and actions to heal us and keep us questing.